MIGHTY MORPHIN POWER RANGERS™

IT'S MORPHIN TIME!

By William McCay

A PARACHUTE PRESS BOOK

A PARACHUTE PRESS BOOK
Parachute Press, Inc.
156 Fifth Avenue
New York, NY 10010

Creative Consultant: Cheryl Saban.

With special thanks to Cheryl Saban, Sheila Dennen, Debi Young, and
Sherry Stack.

Printed in the U.S.A.
May 1994
ISBN: 0-938753-78-9
  C D E F G H I J

PROLOGUE

The Battle Begins

Long ago, Good and Evil met in a great battle. The wizard Zordon led the forces of Good. He fought against Rita Repulsa, who wanted to rule the universe with her forces of Evil.

Both sides fought hard, but the war ended in a tie. So Zordon and

Rita made a deal. They would both flip coins to decide who was the winner. Whoever made the best three tosses out of five would win. The loser would be locked away forever.

Of course, Zordon did not want to risk the safety of the universe on five coins—unless they were magic coins! So with his five special coins, Zordon won the coin toss. But Rita had one last trick up her sleeve. Before she was locked away, she trapped Zordon in another dimension. Now he must stay inside a column of green light at his command center forever and ever.

Rita and her wicked friends

were dropped into an intergalactic prison and flung through space. They crashed into a tiny moon of a faraway planet. After ten thousand years, space travelers found the prison and opened it. Rita and her servants, Baboo, Squatt, Goldar, and Finster, were free!

Rita hadn't changed one bit in ten thousand years. She began planning to take over the universe again. And she saw her first target in the sky above—Earth!

When Zordon heard of Rita's escape, he put his master plan into action. He called Alpha 5, the robot running his command center on Earth. "Teleport to us five of the wildest, most willful humans in the area," he commanded.

"No!" Alpha 5 said. "Not... teenagers!"

But Alpha 5 did as he was told, and teleported five teenagers to the command center.

"Earth is under attack by the evil Rita Repulsa," Zordon explained to the teenagers. "I have chosen you to battle her and save the planet. Each of you will receive great powers drawn from the spirits of the dinosaurs."

Zordon gave each teenager a belt with a magic coin—a Power Morpher! "When you are in danger, raise your Power Morpher to

4

the sky," Zordon instructed. "Then call out the name of your dinosaur and you will morph into a mighty fighter—a Power Ranger!

"Jason, you will be the Red Ranger, with the power of the great tyrannosaurus," Zordon explained. "Trini will be the Yellow Ranger, with the force of the saber-toothed tiger. Zack will be the Black Ranger, with the power of the mastodon. Kimberly will be the Pink Ranger, with pterodactyl power. And Billy will be the Blue Ranger, backed by the power of the triceratops."

For big problems, the Power Rangers could call upon Dinozords—giant robots they piloted into battle. And if things got really tough, the Dinozords could combine together to make a super-robot—a mighty Megazord!

Power Rangers, dinosaur spirits, and robots—together, these incredible forces would protect the Earth.

But the teenagers had to follow Zordon's three rules:

1. Never use your powers for selfish reasons.

2. Never make a fight worse—unless Rita forces you.

3. Always keep your identities secret. No one must ever find out that you are a Mighty Morphin Power Ranger!

CHAPTER 1

"This is gonna be an awesome Food Fair!" Zack said as he and Trini dashed into the Angel Grove Youth Center, balancing two trays full of fresh vegetables.

"Yeah, we get to try great foods from different countries, and we'll raise lots of money for the kids,"

Trini added cheerfully.

Kimberly grinned as she carried a big chocolate cake behind her friends. "Just like Trini. She loves to help people," Kimberly said to Jason, who was standing right beside her.

But these teenagers helped out with more than just the Food Fair. Kimberly, Jason, Trini, and their friends Zack and Billy had special powers. Whenever the Earth was under attack by Rita Repulsa, an evil empress from another world, they became a super fighting team—the Mighty Morphin Power Rangers!

Jason carried a heavy box of hamburger patties. He and

Kimberly were in charge of the American food stand. "Well, it *is* for a really good cause," he said. "Everybody from school will come to the fair. If they buy enough food, we can buy playground equipment for the day-care center and preschool. They really need it." He looked around at all the kids wearing clothes from many different lands. Even Ernie, who ran the center's juice bar, was helping out. He wanted to show off his Hawaiian cooking. He wore a brightly colored shirt and a crown made of flowers.

"I'm glad we signed up for the American booth," Jason said to Kimberly. "At least we get to wear

9

our regular clothes."

Kimberly laughed. Her shoulder-length brown hair was pulled up into a high ponytail, and she had on a white sweater and pink jeans. She looked at Jason's red shirt and pants. "I'd say we look like all-American kids," she said.

The teenagers stopped to say hello to Mr. Caplan, the principal of Angel Grove High School. Mr. Caplan had volunteered to help run the Food Fair. He was a skinny man with two-toned hair, gray on the sides and dark on top. "We have a big crowd outside," he said. "Looks like the Cultural Food Fair will be a success."

Mr. Caplan bent over the cake

that Kimberly was holding. "Chocolate's my favorite." He reached out to scoop up some icing for a taste.

"Mr. Caplan, you have to buy it first!" Kimberly exclaimed.

Billy ran up to them, holding out a huge collecting jar. His blue eyes twinkled behind his glasses. "I believe that cake costs twenty dollars," he said.

Mr. Caplan quickly pulled back. "I wasn't that hungry anyway," he said with a sigh.

Just then, the loudspeaker announced that the Food Fair was open. Lots of students from the high school came crowding in. The Power Rangers rushed to their places. Trini was selling Japanese food. She wore a yellow silk kimono and her long dark hair was pulled back in a matching bow. "Try some of these vegetables," she said.

"They're stir-fried," Billy said as he collected money from the kids in line.

Zack had on a cool yellow, red, and green pullover at his booth of African food. "We've got some good stuff you're going to like," he told the kids.

"Hey, try the good old American cheeseburger!" shouted Kimberly.

Jason held up a tray of burgers. "Come and get 'em! Fresh off the grill!" he called out.

Mr. Caplan looked very, very pleased. "This is just what I like to see! Good, healthy community spirit."

Off in a corner, Bulk made a face. The straggly brown-haired goof-off turned to his nasty friends. "This is just what I like to see. A bunch of goody-goodies about to get creamed...by pies, that is."

He and his pals walked to a table full of desserts. "Hey," Bulk whispered as he picked up a cream pie. "I bet I can hit the principal!"

He threw. But the pie missed Mr. Caplan—almost! Gooey

cream caught the principal's hair, yanking it off. It was a wig! The pie whizzed on and hit a skinny guy with dark hair—Bulk's best friend, Skull. He blinked through a face full of cream. Then Skull yelled, "FOOD FIGHT!"

The kids in the room went crazy. Tacos, salads, and chow mein flew through the air.

Mr. Caplan finally found his wig. It was floating in a punch bowl. He clapped it on his head and hid behind a table.

"We've got to stop this!" Jason yelled.

"We've got to save the Food Fair!" Trini cried.

Jason sprang into action after

the main troublemaker. Bulk was about to throw another cream pie. Jason grabbed a string of hot dogs and swung them over his head. He whirled the food like a karate weapon. Bulk stopped and stared at Jason. The pie slipped. It landed on his own head!

Bulk grabbed two cans of whipped cream to squirt at Jason.

"Yo, big guy," Zack called. "Why don't you chill with that?" Bulk turned and aimed the cans at Zack. Zack whipped off his apron and pretended it was a bullfighter's cape. "Toro! Toro!" he yelled.

Bulk charged, but in one smooth move, Zack leaped aside. Bulk flopped onto Ernie's table.

He slid into trays of pineapples and fresh fruit. Then he hit the bowl of punch. It slopped out— and soaked Mr. Caplan.

"That's it!" the principal yelled.

All the kids skidded to a stop. They knew they were in trouble. Big trouble!

CHAPTER 2

"OOOH-OOOH-OOOH!" Rita Repulsa groaned. In Rita's fortress on the moon, there was lots of screaming. "I'm sick! My head hurts! I have a sore throat! My stomach. Oooh, my stomach!" she cried.

Rita's groans rang through the

main tower. Her chief helpers, Squatt and Baboo, paid no attention. They were busy fighting over the magic telescope Rita used to spy on the Power Rangers. Rita's evil plan was to take over the Earth. All that stood in her way were the Power Rangers!

"C'mon, Squatt!" Baboo said. He was a creature that looked like a cross between a monkey and bat. His thin lips twisted in a frown. "Let me have a turn! What are they doing down there?"

Squatt's big, ugly, grinning green face was glued to the eyepiece. "Looks like they're having some kind of a food festival. Yum!"

"Really?" Baboo danced back and forth. His wings rattled as he tried to get around Squatt. "Let me see! Let me see!"

Suddenly Rita interrupted them. She staggered toward them, her fancy red and gold cloak dragging along the stairs. She was making awful faces. "Oooh, Baboo," she moaned, "I feel terrible." She slid down the wall to sit on the floor.

Baboo's main job around the fortress was buttering up Rita. He knew exactly what to say. "Oh, no, Evil One!" he whimpered. "You can't be sick!"

"Don't tell me I can't," Rita said, drooping. Then she popped up to yell right in her servant's face. "Because I *am*, you dolt!"

Baboo realized he hadn't said the right thing. And that was a problem, because he worked for a witch who could turn people into frogs. "Yes, yes," he babbled. "Of course you are, Your Badness."

"You don't know about bad!" Rita squawked. "I haven't felt this horrible since Zordon locked me away."

"I know, Your Awfulness," Baboo quickly said. "I was there, too. But it wasn't so bad after the first thousand years."

"Are you arguing with me?"

"Oh, no—that is, I never—I mean—" Baboo crouched down

with his hands over his head. "Please don't zap me or turn me into something icky!"

He peeked out from between his fingers. "Maybe you'd feel better if you thought about all the nasty things you can do once you conquer Earth."

"Hey," Squatt said. "I've got something to cheer you up." He stood in front of the telescope.

"Cheer me up?" Rita stomped over and pushed Squatt aside. "Let me see."

She looked through the telescope. "Uck! Food!" she yelled. "Now I really feel sick! Look at those kids! They're acting like disgusting pigs!"

Rita turned away, sicker than ever. Then she stopped. "Pigs," she said slowly. "That gives me an idea! If they like food fights, I'll give them a fight!"

She zoomed to Finster's workshop. Finster was Rita's chief monster-maker. When he placed small clay statues in his Monstermatic, they turned into evil, living creatures. The pale and droopy alien sat squishing clay in the shape of a monster. "Almost finished," he said.

"Forget about that," Rita said. "Make me a monster, but not your usual. This has to be special."

"All my monsters are special—" Finster began. He quickly shut up when he saw Rita raise her magic staff.

"I want a pig," Rita said. "Make him big and fat, a pudgy pig!"

"I did make a pudgy pig, but it's not my best work," Finster said. He pointed to a chubby model pig that lay at the top of a bin marked "Rejects."

"Then *make* it your best work!" Rita shrieked. "Make sure he has a big appetite. I want him to eat all the food on Earth, starting in Angel Grove!"

Finster put the dumpy little model on the track leading to his Monster-matic. He pushed a lever on the side of the machine. The track started to move, and the pig model rolled in. *HOOT! CLANK! HOOT! CLUNK!* The whole contraption began to wiggle. Steam hissed. Tubes jiggled.

Then, *KABOOM!* The monster appeared in a cloud of smoke. It was a pig, all right, with a big, pudgy face. In fact, it was almost all face. The pig-out monster had arms, legs, and a huge head. It wore a black helmet, and its mouth had to be a yard wide.

Rita smiled an evil smile. "Go to Earth," she told the monster. "Eat everything in sight!"

CHAPTER 3

Back at the Angel Grove Youth Center everyone was quiet—except Mr. Caplan. He began roaring angrily, his wig still dripping wet. "Look at this mess!" he shouted.

The big room was in pretty sad shape. There was food on the

walls, on the floors, and on the kids. Kimberly even saw some chow mein stuck to the ceiling.

That wasn't the worst thing. The kids had played with the food, but they hadn't bought much. That meant no money for the day-care center and pre-school. Bulk's food fight had spoiled more than just food.

"Our Food Fair is ruined!" an unhappy Mr. Caplan said. His angry eyes glared at the Power Rangers. "You really should be ashamed of yourselves!"

Jason felt pretty upset, too. "But, Mr. Caplan—" he began, stepping forward.

"No buts!" shouted the principal. He grabbed a broom and handed it to Jason. "Here, you're in charge of the cleanup!" Then he stormed off.

At the word "cleanup," most of the teenagers stampeded for the door. "Don't go!" Trini called after them. "We can save some of this food! At least we could sell what we have left."

But most of the kids were already gone.

"Raw deal," said Zack. His usually cheerful smile was missing. "We tried to stop this mess. Now we're stuck doing the rubbing and scrubbing." He looked around the room, shaking his head "This isn't a job for a cleanup crew.

This is a job for superheroes."

Jason slowly shook his head. "Remember what Zordon told us," he said quietly. "We can't use our powers for little things."

Just then, the communicator on Jason's wrist beeped. He looked around. There were still a few kids hanging out.

"Come on," he told his friends. They ducked behind a booth. Then Jason tapped a button. "Come in, Zordon."

"Power Rangers," the wizard's deep voice came from the tiny radio. "I need you at the command center immediately."

"We're on our way." Jason and the other Power Rangers touched their communicators. Instantly they vanished in a flash of light—and materialized inside Zordon's command center.

Big super-science machines jammed the huge, dark room. The viewing globe was already on. It showed a picture of Rita's monster attacking a supermarket in downtown Angel Grove.

The Power Rangers watched as the pig began gobbling. It scooped up a pile of grapefruits. They disappeared into its big mouth, skins and all. Then came a crate of melons. It crunched them down, rinds, crate, and all! It was the same with the candy bars the pig ate next. It didn't unwrap them. The monster just stuffed its mouth and swallowed.

"What a pig!" Kimberly cried.

"SHLOMP! GULP!" went the monster. In seconds, the pig ate everything in the store!

"This dude needs a serious diet," said Zack.

"Doesn't it ever stop?" Trini asked as she stared in horror.

The image of Zordon's face floated in a tube of glowing green light. He said, "It appears that Rita has unleashed a hungry pig monster upon the Earth. Its sole purpose is to eat."

"If this dude keeps this up, it will eventually eat everything!" Zack said.

**"This is gonna be an awesome Food Fair!"
says Zack.**

Bulk has some messy tricks to play on Jason and his friends!

Jason, Trini, and Zack wonder what Bulk is up to this time.

"FOOD FIGHT!"

Ernie is disappointed—the Food Fair is ruined!

"I need you at the command center immediately," Zordon calls on Jason's communicator.

Billy, Zack, Kimberly, Trini, and Alpha learn all about Rita's pig monster!

"Guys," Jason said. "It's morphin time!"

This pig is ready to eat—everything!

"This monster is sure to destroy the Power Rangers for good!" Finster cries.

"You're finished, pig!" exclaims the Red Ranger.

Alpha 5 gets ready to do some cosmic Food Fair cooking of his own!

Zordon nodded. "I calculate that the pig will consume the entire supply of food on Earth in forty-eight hours. It must be stopped!"

"It could use a good workout!" Kimberly joked.

The voice of Alpha 5 came from behind them. "Greetings, dudes and dudettes!" The little robot wore a chef's hat on his shiny metal head. "I thought I'd give you a hand with the food for the fair."

Zordon frowned. "Later, Alpha," the wizard said. "Our Power Rangers have work to do."

"Guys," Jason said. "It's morphin time!"

The teens held up their Power Morphers. Just as Zordon had taught them, they called upon the spirits of the ancient dinosaurs.

"Mastodon!" cried Zack.

"Pterodactyl!" cried Kimberly.

"Triceratops!" cried Billy.

"Saber-toothed Tiger!" cried Trini.

"Tyrannosaurus!" cried Jason.

In a flash, the five morphed into—Power Rangers!

Outfitted in their sleek jump-suits and helmets, they cried, "Let's do it!" Then they vanished.

CHAPTER 4

Seconds later, the Power Rangers teleported to downtown Angel Grove. They saw the pig-out monster swallowing its way through a candy store.

The monster grunted when it spotted them. It came outside and leaped ten floors to the roof of a building.

Jason, the Red Ranger, raised a powerful fist. "Okay, you're finished, pig!"

"Yeah, porker," Zack, the Black Ranger, shouted, his knees bent in a karate stance. "The feast is over."

"That pig is *so* disgusting!" cried the Pink Ranger. Kimberly couldn't get over how gross the monster was.

Trini, the Yellow Ranger, called a challenge. "Come down and fight like a pig!"

With a wild squeal, the pig bounded down. Magic weapons appeared in the Power Rangers' hands. Together, they charged—and missed the pig! The monster looked big, fat, and stupid, but it was also fast and strong.

When Jason swung his Power Sword, the pig ducked. When Billy jabbed with his Power Lance, the monster dodged. The pig didn't miss with its strikes, though. It hit the Power Rangers with pig punches. Sparks flew, and the Power Rangers tumbled backward.

Just as Kimberly and Trini jumped to their feet, the pig blew a mouthful of steam at them. The two Power Rangers felt themselves being pulled forward. Their weapons were sucked into the pig's huge, open mouth!

"Trini, it's eating my Power

Bow!" Kimberly cried.

"My Power Daggers, too!" Trini shouted.

For a second, it looked as if the pig would swallow them, too!

Trini ducked, and Kimberly triple-flipped out of the way.

Billy stabbed at the pig. But its big mouth just slurped up Billy's Power Lance—and nearly swallowed Billy's arm along with it! Then Zack's Power Ax was chowed down with one gulp.

From her fortress on the moon, Rita gloated. "Ha ha! The Power Rangers' weapons went down the hatch!"

Finster smiled. His "reject" pig

was turning out to be the best monster he had ever made. "This monster is sure to destroy the Power Rangers for good," he said.

Back on Earth, Jason slashed at the monster with his Power Sword. The pig hopped away. Jason sliced, but the pig blocked! The sword bounced high in the air. When it came down, the pig-out monster gobbled it up!

"Oh, man, my sword!" Jason yelled. He tried a karate attack. The pig was faster, and kicked Jason away. The other four Power Rangers helped him up. Then they lined up to charge again.

But the pig had other plans. A beam of light shot out of its snout. The Power Rangers tried to dodge it, but couldn't. The beam started to spin them around.

Faster and faster they whirled, until they became just streaks of color.

"WHOOOAH!" they yelled. Their voices began to echo. And they were gone!

CHAPTER 5

The heroes were trapped in the whirling blur. Then suddenly the spinning stopped. Five confused teenagers were dumped on the ground. They were in Angel Grove Park, miles from where they had fought the pig! They also weren't Power Rangers anymore. All five of them were dressed in their Food Fair clothes.

Zack rubbed a hand through his curly dark hair. "What a weird way to travel."

"This is too strange," Jason said as he slowly got to his feet.

Then Jason's communicator beeped. "Power Rangers!" Zordon called. "While you were caught in the pig's spin-beam, he smelled his way to your Food Fair and is on the attack."

"What can he do at the Food Fair—it's already a mess," said Kimberly.

"My sensors show me that after you left, many of the kids came back to the fair and cleaned up," explained Zordon. "The fair did go on—until now!"

"Come on!" Jason shouted. "There's no time to lose!"

While the Power Rangers raced to the Food Fair, the pig-out monster was busy shoveling everything it could find into its mouth. "Whahoo! Waaaaow!" it yelled.

A basket full of chips disappeared down its big throat. The monster shoved its snout into a tray of burgers. It sucked them down, too. The pig ran from booth to booth, snorting. Then it bumped into Bulk.

Bulk pushed up his nose to look like a pig. "Snort! Snort!" he shouted. Bulk and Skull laughed.

The big pig didn't like that. It began to roar. Bulk and Skull took off running faster than they ever had before. The pig kept eating.

Ernie hid behind the table with his ruined Hawaiian food. "Where are the Power Rangers when you need them?" he cried. When the monster came his way, he ran right out the door!

"More food! More food!" the pig yelled. The next booth in line had a sign that warned "Hot! Hot! Hot!" in big red letters. Pig-out sniffed a basket of spicy peppers. "Yuck!" cried the monster. It spilled the basket and went for a bowl of popcorn instead. When the pig finished the last kernels, it simply vanished.

A second later, the Power Rangers came running in.

"Eyuuuuuu, what a mess!" Kimberly said.

Bowls and dishes, broken glasses, and plates were tossed all around. Even the tables were turned over.

"Man, it ate everything in sight," Zack said. "Mr. Caplan's going to flip his wig—again."

Jason shook his head. "We've got to stop that pig."

"But how?" Kimberly asked. "That thing just swallowed our weapons."

Trini stared thoughtfully at one booth in the corner. "Hey, wait a minute," she said. "Do you guys see what I see?"

She led the way to the "Hot! Hot! Hot!" booth and said, "That pig ate everything in sight—but it didn't even touch the hot stuff!"

Kimberly shrugged. "Well, it must not like spicy food."

"Correct," Billy said. He was the class brain, and Trini knew he had a plan. "Perhaps we can use that information to defeat the monster."

"How?" Zack asked.

"Well, why not lure the animal with food it likes?" Billy said. He picked up a hot pepper and smiled. "But we stick a piece of this pepper inside."

Kimberly grinned. "Morphi-nominal idea, Billy!"

Jason smiled, too. "And we make the pig so sick, it coughs up our weapons."

"Right!" said Billy.

Trini scooped up the basket of peppers. "I'll bring the hot stuff," she said.

Jason tapped on his communicator. "Zordon! We found a way to defeat the pig!"

"We just need to know where it is," Trini added.

Zordon answered immediately. "My sensors tell me that it is terrorizing the food-packing plant. Go now, Power Rangers. And may the power protect you!"

The Power Rangers raised their Power Morphers into the air. They called on the powers of the ancient dinosaurs. "Mastodon!" "Pterodactyl!" "Triceratops!" "Saber-toothed Tiger!" "Tyrannosaurus!" A crackling glow filled the air.

"POWER RANGERS!" the five shouted—and morphed into their super forms.

In a flash they were standing in front of the food-packing plant. They leaped to the roof of a building that overlooked the plant. Inside, the pig was munching away.

The Power Rangers lined up. They held some very odd

weapons in their hands. Jason carried a big steak. Zack had a pie. Billy held a huge pizza. Kimberly's plate held a piece of cake. Trini had a giant hero sandwich.

"Come on, piggy!" Jason yelled. "Free food!"

The pig gave a hungry squeal. It bounded out of the warehouse.

Jason, Zack, Billy, and Kimberly threw down their food. The pig opened its mouth wider and wider. "GULP! GULP! GULP!" It swallowed everything!

"Okay, Trini!" Jason called. "Send down the hot stuff!"

Trini held up a pepper. She slipped it into her hero sandwich.

"One red-hot pepper coming up!" Trini stepped forward. "Hey, pig," she called. "You hungry? Catch!"

Then Trini threw the long hero sandwich like a spear. It flew straight down the pig's throat!

CHAPTER 6

"**Huh? Whaaa!**" the pig squawked. This new snack didn't go down well! It burned, fiery hot! The pig's mouth flew open. A cloud of pink, red, and white smoke poured out.

The pig made awful noises at the top of its lungs. "Wahoo-hoo-

hoo-hoo!" it cried.

The monster started coughing up all sorts of fruit and food. A bunch of grapes flew out. Billy's pizza bounced out. Out popped a bunch of candy bars, still in their wrappers.

"All right!" the Power Rangers yelled.

"Gross," Kimberly said.

"It's working!" Trini said.

"Uck!" said Pig-out.

Jason's Power Sword and Billy's Power Lance flew out of its mouth.

The Red and Blue Rangers leaped high. They caught their weapons in midair.

"Ook!" moaned the unhappy

monster, holding its sides.

Now it coughed up Zack's Power Ax and Trini's Power Daggers. The Black Ranger caught his ax. The Yellow Ranger grabbed up her knives.

"Urk!" went the pig. Kimberly's bow whizzed out. The Pink Ranger caught it.

Rita's pudgy pig wasn't pudgy anymore. It looked like a squeezed-out tube of toothpaste. Squeal after unhappy squeal filled the air. The pig staggered around. Little puffs of smoke came out of its mouth.

The Power Rangers charged!

Zack and Billy soared through the air. They whizzed over the pig's head. The Power Ax and Power Lance banged against the pig's helmet. Sparks flew.

Now Jason and Billy faced the pig. The Yellow and Pink Rangers ran up behind them, leaped, and bounced off their shoulders. Zooming high through the sky, they aimed their weapons, and *KA-BAM!* Lots more sparks flew as arrows and daggers crashed into the pig.

Then Jason leaped at the pig, his Power Sword high. *Crash!* He slammed it on the monster's helmet. It gave a loud, unhappy squeal. Then it fell on its back.

"Let's finish this porker!" Jason shouted.

"Right!" cried the rest of the team.

They threw their weapons into the sky. The ax, bow, lance, and daggers magically joined together. Jason leaped up and added his sword. It locked in place, and the whole weapon glowed. Now Jason held the mighty Power Gun!

The Red Ranger landed on the ground. He aimed the magic gun, and fired! Multicolored rays shot from the weapon.

"Waah! Hoo-hoo-hoo!" Pig-out cried as the rays hit. The ground shook. A blinding glare surround-ed the monster. It yelled louder, hopping around. Pink and purple lightning bolts flew around the pig. Then the Power Rangers saw a cloud of smoke and a shower of sparks—and the pig was gone!

"I bet that lowered his cholesterol!" Kimberly laughed.

"Hey, Rita!" Trini yelled up to the sky. "You'll have to do better than that if you want to beat us!"

Up on the moon, Rita was *very* unhappy. She glared at Finster. "You fool! Your monster was worthless!"

Finster began to get worried. "But I warned you he wasn't my best work," he whined.

Baboo didn't want to get

blamed for anything. He began hitting Squatt. "This is all your fault," he said loudly. "You always mess things up."

Rita growled.

"Now, now, my queen." Finster felt really nervous now. "Please don't yell at me and turn me into a toad. Please! I beg you!"

Rita stomped around. "I lost again and it's all your fault!" She turned to the squabbling Baboo and Squatt. "As for you two, shut up!"

She stared up at the Earth, high above. Then she shook her fist. "How can anyone conquer the world with these nitwits!" she complained.

On Earth, the Power Rangers looked just like ordinary teenagers again. But they were still excited from winning their big fight. Jason laughed as they walked into the youth center. "We really gave it to Rita this time," he said.

"Yeah!" Zack kicked at a pretend enemy. "We were morphinominal!"

Kimberly pointed at the room. "But what about the Food Fair?"

Trini sighed as she looked at the disaster. "Do you guys think we made enough money for the playground equipment before the pig monster trashed the place?"

Jason's communicator beeped.

"I see you finished your mission, Power Rangers," Zordon said.

Jason grinned. "Yeah. We sent that pudgy pig to the fat farm!"

Back at the command center, Zordon smiled. "Congratulations," he said. "Well done."

Alpha 5 walked up to Zordon. He still wore his chef's hat and carried three trays of sandwiches. "I have figured out a way to defeat that pesky pig," the robot said.

. "Whoa, Alpha," Jason said into his radio. "I think we have the problem under control."

"Yeah," Zack said. "That pig is sausage, man!"

Trini didn't sound as happy as her friends. "But he ruined our

Food Fair."

"Oh, that's too bad," Alpha said. "Maybe I can help."

The sandwich trays in his hands glowed. Then they disappeared. A second later, Billy, Zack, and Jason each held a tray. "Hey, thanks, Alpha!" Zack said.

Just then, Mr. Caplan entered the youth center. The principal's suit was stained from the punch. His squashed wig covered only half of his bald head.

"I'm sorry for blaming you kids for the fight. I know you weren't responsible," Mr. Caplan said. "And I've got good news—we almost have enough money for the playground equipment."

Trini flashed him a huge smile. "How much more do we need?" she asked.

"Twenty dollars," the principal replied.

Trini pointed to the trays of food.

"Hmmm." Mr. Caplan gave the sandwiches a hungry look. "How much for one?"

"Exactly twenty dollars," Trini told him.

The principal stared. "Twenty dollars?"

"For the playground equipment," Trini said sweetly.

"Well, it's for a good cause, and I'm starving," he said, handing Trini the money. He picked up a hero sandwich and took a big bite. But he didn't see the hot pepper dangling from it.

Billy tried to warn him. "Be careful, it's a little bit—"

He didn't have to finish the sentence. Mr. Caplan's cheeks blew out and he gasped, "Ohhh! Water! I need water!"

Kimberly ran to a nearby table. She grabbed a pitcher full of water and handed it over.

Mr. Caplan opened his lips wide and tilted the pitcher. Water poured down his mouth and over his face. It splashed on top of his head and washed his wig away!

The principal didn't seem to mind. "Ah," he said after his long drink. "A little hot." He smacked his lips. "But not bad."

Mr. Caplan began to laugh. And after a second, the Power Rangers joined in, too.